Hail to the Chief

BY CALLISTA GINGRICH

ILLUSTRATED BY SUSAN ARCIERO

★ ★ ★ ★ ★ Acknowledgments ★ ★ ★ ★ ★

Thank you to the incredible people who have made this book possible.

I especially want to thank Susan Arciero, whose outstanding illustrations have once again brought Ellis the Elephant to life.

The team at Regnery Kids has made writing *Hail to the Chief* a real pleasure. Thanks to Marji Ross and Cheryl Barnes for their insightful and creative contributions. Regnery has been remarkable in turning this book into a reality.

My sincere gratitude goes to our staff at Gingrich Productions, including Ross Worthington, Bess Kelly, Christina Maruna, Woody Hales, Audrey Bird, and John Hines. Their support has been invaluable.

Finally, I'd like to thank my husband, Newt. His enthusiasm for the Ellis the Elephant series has been my source of inspiration.

Regnery Kids™ is a trademark of Salem Communications Holding Corporation;
Regnery® is a registered trademark of Salem Communications Holding Corporation

Cataloging-in-Publication date on file with the Library of Congress
ISBN 978-1-62157-479-8

Published in the United States by
Regnery Kids
An imprint of Regnery Publishing
A Division of Salem Media Group
300 New Jersey Ave NW
Washington, DC 20001
www.RegneryKids.com

Manufactured in the United States of America
10 9 8 7 6 5 4 3 2 1

Books are available in quantity for promotional or premium use.
For information on discounts and terms, please visit our website: www.Regnery.com.

Distributed to the trade by
Perseus Distribution
250 West 57th Street
New York, NY 10107

Dedicated to our American presidents
who have led this exceptional nation.

★ ★ ★ ★ ★

The American president has a great task,
a job as exciting as anyone could ask.
Elected to uphold America's laws,
the commander in chief defends freedom's cause.

Ellis the Elephant knew our country was blessed
with exceptional leaders who stood up to the test.
He was eager to meet the presidents of the past
and learn how they governed a nation so vast.

Ellis had heard of George Washington before—
the man who led the Revolutionary War.
After the war it was General Washington's fate
to lead the new nation he fought to create.

As president, Washington was ready to serve,
defending the freedoms he pledged to preserve.
Our country's first leader set the standard indeed
for future presidents who would follow his lead.

Thomas Jefferson was a Founding Father of our nation.
He wrote of independence in a famous Declaration.
With clarity and passion, this document explained
how our God-given rights must always be maintained.

As president, Jefferson had a grand vision
and boldly made an important decision.
His Louisiana Purchase added new land
and opened the West for America to expand.

Known as the Father of the Constitution,
James Madison drafted a brilliant solution.
As president, Madison had challenges galore
when a British invasion took our country to war.

At the Battle of Baltimore, Ellis had no doubt
we'd win the War of 1812 and kick the British out!
Here the "Star Spangled Banner" waved high for all to see,
and inspired our anthem by Francis Scott Key.

Andrew Jackson captured the public's admiration—
a "man of the people" with a strong reputation.
He vowed to remember his own humble start,
and took every American's needs to heart.

But Jackson learned the challenge of fame and success
when his inaugural party became a real mess.
Thousands crowded the White House and made such a clamor—
a major departure from its usual glamour!

Abraham Lincoln bravely and wisely presided
over a nation in crisis and deeply divided.
A fight over slavery caused the country to split
and the Civil War started when the South tried to quit.

The conflict was awful, and took a great toll.
So at Gettysburg, Lincoln rose to console.
The Union Army fought long and hard to ensure
that this fragile young nation could "long endure."

America was filled with many beautiful places,
with mountains and valleys and wide open spaces.
President Teddy Roosevelt cherished conservation,
and wanted to preserve the best land for the nation.

Roosevelt set aside millions of acres of land,
and traveled the country to see them firsthand.
On one camping trip, he couldn't help but remark
on the beauty of Yosemite National Park.

As president, Woodrow Wilson decided to send
U.S. soldiers to bring World War I to an end.
When all sides agreed that the fighting would cease,
he sought to ensure a long-lasting peace.

Ellis learned that Wilson advanced a greater cause:
that all nations would agree to the same set of laws.
In Paris, he argued for a new organization,
an international body called the League of Nations.

Before long World War II suddenly began,
and Franklin D. Roosevelt was just the right man.
He spoke out so the American people could hear
that through war and hardship, they had "nothing to fear."

Through "fireside chats" he shared America's plight
and gave people the courage to continue the fight.
Month by month, Allied forces pushed on to Berlin,
certain this was a struggle they'd eventually win.

At long last the Second World War was won,
but America's job was not yet done.
Communism threatened freedom once more
and this, Ellis learned, was called the Cold War.

President Harry Truman proposed an alliance
to unite the free nations in strong defiance.
The NATO agreement left many impressed
with the strength and resolve of the unified West.

General Dwight Eisenhower, best known as "Ike,"
was a president that most Americans liked.
In World War II, he earned the people's respect—
and soon won their hearts as president-elect.

Ike made it his mission to plan and create
a nationwide network of new interstates.
These wide open roads kept America thriving—
and Ellis imagined the thrill of fast driving!

The early 1960s were a hopeful time,
for a courageous leader who served in his prime.
John F. Kennedy asked citizens to volunteer
to improve and preserve the nation they held dear.

Ellis was inspired by Kennedy's bold themes,
and how he challenged Americans to dream big dreams.
He sent men to the Moon within a few short years
to discover and explore its vast new frontiers.

Lyndon Johnson's years were anything but calm,
with unrest at home and war in Vietnam.
While the times made his job especially tough,
President Johnson did some important stuff.

With Martin Luther King, he fought discrimination
to keep a founding promise of our great nation.
Together they were determined to win crucial fights
that guaranteed to everyone equal civil rights.

Ronald Reagan had faith in the American way,
knowing that freedom, not fear, would carry the day.
Ellis learned that Reagan pursued one major goal:
to liberate the world from Soviet control.

Reagan went to Berlin, a city split in two,
with one thing he insisted the Soviets do.
When he called on their leaders to "tear down this wall,"
his words marked the start of the communist fall.

Thinking back on all the presidents he observed,
Ellis was so grateful for those who had served.
Throughout our history, they gave what was needed
and strived to ensure that our country succeeded.

Each had accepted a great responsibility,
and done the job to the best of their ability.
Ellis had tremendous respect and admiration
for the presidents who'd led this exceptional nation.

★ ★ ★ ★ ★ Resources ★ ★ ★ ★ ★

1. George Washington (1789–1797)

On April 30, 1789, George Washington took his inaugural oath to become the first president of the United States. Before he became president, Washington was commander in chief of the Continental Army during the Revolutionary War. For these reasons and for the many precedents he set as president, Washington is known as the "Father of our Country." Today, you can still visit Washington's beautiful estate in Mount Vernon, Virginia.

2. John Adams (1797–1801)

Before becoming the second president of the United States in 1797, John Adams served as George Washington's vice president, making him the first person to hold that office. He was also one of the most important of the Founding Fathers for his role in both the American Revolution and the Constitutional Convention. Adams and his wife, Abigail, were the first residents of the White House in Washington, D.C.

3. Thomas Jefferson (1801–1809)

In 1776, at the age of thirty-three, Thomas Jefferson drafted the Declaration of Independence at the Second Continental Congress in Philadelphia. His famous preamble states that "all men are created equal," and "are endowed by their Creator" with rights to "life, liberty and the pursuit of happiness." In 1801 Jefferson was inaugurated as the third president of the United States. He made the Louisiana Purchase in 1803 and authorized the Lewis and Clark Expedition in 1804, opening up the West for expansion.

4. James Madison (1809–1817)

James Madison is known as the "Father of the Constitution" for his crucial role in drafting the document and arguing for its adoption in *The Federalist Papers*. As president of the United States, Madison was faced with the War of 1812, a three-year conflict with Great Britain. During the Battle of Baltimore, one of the pivotal engagements of the war, Francis Scott Key wrote the poem "Defense of Fort McHenry" as he watched the bombardment. This poem was later set to music and retitled the "Star Spangled Banner" when it was officially declared our national anthem in 1931.

5. James Monroe (1817–1825)

James Monroe was America's fifth president and the last Founding Father to serve. As president, Monroe oversaw significant westward expansion and purchased the state of Florida from Spain. His greatest legacy was the "Monroe Doctrine" in 1823 which became the basis of American foreign policy.

6. John Quincy Adams (1825–1829)

John Quincy Adams, the first president who was a son of a former president, was also an accomplished diplomat and influential secretary of state. During his presidency, he dramatically reduced the national debt and worked to promote education, art, and science.

7. Andrew Jackson (1829–1837)

Andrew Jackson's service as a general in the War of 1812 earned him national fame as a war hero, and eventually propelled him to the presidency in 1829. As the first president who came from humble beginnings, Jackson was known as a "man of the people." In fact, he was such a popular figure that thousands of people swarmed the White House after his inaugural ceremony, in the hopes of congratulating the new president. The building became so crowded that Jackson had to escape to a hotel across the street.

8. Martin Van Buren (1837–1841)

Martin Van Buren was the eighth president of the United States and a skilled political organizer who helped forge the Democratic Party. In previous administrations, he served as both vice president and secretary of state. The most significant event of Van Buren's presidency was the financial crisis of 1837, which caused an economic depression.

9. William Henry Harrison (1841)

William Henry Harrison served the shortest presidential term in American history. He was elected on the strength of his reputation as a military officer. Just thirty-two days after he was inaugurated, however, Harrison died from complications of pneumonia. He was said to have contracted the illness as a result of riding in the rain during his inaugural parade.

10. John Tyler (1841–1845)

John Tyler ascended to the presidency after the death of his predecessor, William Henry Harrison. Tyler was a strong supporter of states' rights and free trade. He sought aggressively to expand the United States territorially, with a particular focus on Texas, which he finally succeeded in annexing at the end of his term in office.

11. James K. Polk (1845–1849)

James K. Polk was the eleventh president of the United States and the only one to have previously served as Speaker of the U.S. House of Representatives. A protégé of Andrew Jackson, Polk also served as governor of Tennessee. As president, he acquired the Oregon Territory for the United States. He was also commander in chief during the Mexican-American War (a result of the annexation of Texas), and was instrumental in acquiring California and New Mexico.

12. Zachary Taylor (1849–1850)

After serving as a general in the United States Army and becoming a national hero during the Mexican-American War, Zachary Taylor was elected president. From the start of his administration, Taylor was faced with growing tensions over slavery between the North and the South. His presidency did not last long, however. He died of a sudden illness after just one year in office.

★ ★ ★ ★ ★ Resources ★ ★ ★ ★ ★

13. Millard Fillmore (1850–1853)

Millard Fillmore became president after the death of Zachary Taylor. As a member of the Whig Party, Fillmore was the last president not to be affiliated with either the Democratic or Republican Party. One of the most significant events of his presidency was the Compromise of 1850, which briefly settled the question of whether new states admitted to the Union would be slave states or free states.

14. Franklin Pierce (1853–1857)

Franklin Pierce came into office during a time of great tension over the issue of slavery. Pierce advocated for passage of the Kansas-Nebraska Act in 1854, which allowed for the matter to be decided by popular sovereignty. When the Act passed, it resulted in a great deal of violence in the territories between pro-slavery forces and abolitionists—an event known as "Bleeding Kansas."

15. James Buchanan (1857–1861)

James Buchanan served as the last president prior to the Civil War. During his presidency, Buchanan was unable to ease the conflict over slavery, and oversaw the southern states driving toward secession. In December 1860, near the end of his administration, South Carolina seceded from the Union, and was soon followed by six other states. Buchanan was the only president to remain a bachelor throughout his life.

16. Abraham Lincoln (1861–1865)

Abraham Lincoln came into office during one of the greatest crises in American history. The nation was split in two over the issue of slavery. In the North, the Union remained loyal to the Constitution. In the South, the Confederate States of America sought to form a new country to preserve the institution of slavery. President Lincoln worked to save the Union through a bloody Civil War. On November 19, 1863, dedicating the Gettysburg National Cemetery in Gettysburg, Pennsylvania, Lincoln delivered his 267-word Gettysburg Address, in which he resolved "that these dead shall not have died in vain—that this nation, under God, shall have a new birth of freedom—and that government of the people, by the people, for the people, shall not perish from the earth." Lincoln was assassinated by John Wilkes Booth on April 15, 1865.

17. Andrew Johnson (1865–1869)

Andrew Johnson ascended to the presidency following the assassination of Abraham Lincoln just days after the surrender at Appomattox, the symbolic end of the Civil War. As a southerner, Johnson was seen as a traitor to the South and a hero in the North for remaining in the U.S. Senate throughout the Civil War. (He was the only senator from a Confederate state who did not resign.) Assuming office immediately after the end of the war, Johnson was left with the difficult task of reconstructing the South and restoring unity to the nation.

18. Ulysses S. Grant (1869–1877)

The former commanding general of the Union Army during the Civil War, Ulysses S. Grant became the eighteenth president of the United States in 1869. At the time of his inauguration, Grant was the youngest president ever at the age of forty-six. During his administration, he established Yellowstone National Park, the first national park, and oversaw the passage of the Fifteenth Amendment to the Constitution, giving African Americans the right to vote.

★ ★ ★ ★ ★ Resources ★ ★ ★ ★ ★

19. Rutherford B. Hayes (1877–1881)

President Rutherford B. Hayes oversaw the end of the difficult period of Reconstruction following the Civil War. He also championed Civil Service reform, with the goal of professionalizing the Civil Service and minimizing the number of government jobs based on patronage or political favors. Hayes had pledged to serve just one term as president, and he retired after four years of service.

20. James A. Garfield (1881)

James A. Garfield served only a few months as president before being assassinated by an angry citizen. During his short time in office, Garfield continued his predecessor's focus on Civil Service reform. He was also devoted to addressing the issue of civil rights, and he appointed a former slave, Frederick Douglass, as recorder of deeds in the District of Columbia.

21. Chester A. Arthur (1881–1885)

Chester A. Arthur became president following the assassination of James Garfield. Arthur devoted much of his presidency to achieving the Civil Service reform that his immediate predecessors had fought for—an effort which culminated with his signing the Pendleton Civil Service Reform Act of 1883, a milestone piece of legislation that continues to shape the federal government today.

22. & 24. Grover Cleveland (1885–1889, 1893–1897)

Grover Cleveland was the first and only president to serve two non-consecutive terms of office, which made him both the twenty-second and the twenty-fourth president of the United States. He was the first Democrat to be elected president after the Civil War. Cleveland was also the only president to get married in the White House. As president, he used his veto power aggressively and generally strengthened the executive branch.

23. Benjamin Harrison (1889–1893)

Benjamin Harrison was the twenty-third president as well as the grandson of a former president, William Henry Harrison. He won office by defeating incumbent President Grover Cleveland. During his administration, Harrison expanded the United States to include Montana, Washington, Idaho, Wyoming, North Dakota, and South Dakota.

25. William McKinley (1897–1901)

William McKinley, a governor of Ohio, ran for president on a platform promoting American prosperity and a stable dollar. He oversaw a significant economic boom and the institution of the gold standard. He was also commander in chief during the Spanish-American War. In 1901, roughly one year into his second term, an anarchist in Buffalo, New York, shot McKinley. He died of complications from his injuries a few days later.

26. Theodore Roosevelt (1901–1909)

Theodore Roosevelt became president following the assassination of his predecessor, William McKinley. The youthful Roosevelt brought vigor to the White House and to the presidency. A committed conservationist, Roosevelt devoted much of his effort to preserving national forests, reserves, and wildlife refuges. This included a large addition to Yosemite National Park. Roosevelt advocated for a greater role for the U.S. in international affairs, overseeing the construction of the Panama Canal and personally winning a Nobel Peace Prize for mediating the Russo-Japanese War.

27. William Howard Taft (1909–1913)

William Howard Taft was the twenty-seventh president of the United States, during a time that required him to navigate new ideological fights between progressives and conservatives. Following his presidency, Taft was appointed chief justice of the Supreme Court. He is the only president to have served in both the executive and judicial branches of the federal government.

28. Woodrow Wilson (1913–1921)

Woodrow Wilson, a former president of Princeton University, led the United States through World War I. He was deeply committed to the League of Nations, a new international organization formed in the aftermath of the war to encourage world peace. Wilson was also an important leader of the progressive movement, and began to implement the progressives' theories about the role of government in shaping society.

29. Warren G. Harding (1921–1923)

Warren G. Harding, a U.S. senator from Ohio, was inaugurated president in 1921, but his term was cut short when he died of a heart attack in 1923. Harding won the election in a landslide, based on the slogan "less government in business and more business in government." Before his death, Harding worked to rebuild the country from the hardships of World War I. Although he died as a very popular president, a number of scandals came to light after his death that tarnished his reputation.

30. Calvin Coolidge (1923–1929)

Calvin Coolidge led the nation through the economic boom of the 1920s. He took office after the sudden death of President Harding. Coolidge brought quiet virtue to the office of the presidency. He promoted smaller government, less spending, lower taxes, and free markets. He also consistently spoke out for the civil rights of African Americans and against racial discrimination.

31. Herbert Hoover (1929–1933)

Herbert Hoover, a former secretary of commerce, was highly regarded for his leadership on humanitarian issues in Europe after World War I. Unfortunately, he took office as president just as the U.S. economy entered the Great Depression. His failure to achieve an economic recovery caused him to lose his bid for reelection four years later.

32. Franklin D. Roosevelt (1933–1945)

Franklin D. Roosevelt was president through one of the most challenging periods in American history—leading the country though the Great Depression and World War II. Roosevelt frequently spoke to the country through his "fireside chats," radio addresses in which he talked about the challenges and hardships facing Americans. Roosevelt's New Deal initiatives were intended to address the effects of the Depression and resulted in a dramatic expansion of federal powers. The only president to be elected four times, Roosevelt died during his fourth term in office.

33. Harry S. Truman (1945–1953)

Harry S. Truman was sworn in as president following the death of President Franklin D. Roosevelt in 1945. Truman led the nation through the end of World War II, and made the difficult decision to drop the atomic bomb on Japan. He also gave the order to integrate the United States armed forces, helping pave the way for the civil rights movement. As president during the early stages of the Cold War, Truman was crucial in organizing the North Atlantic Treaty Organisation to defend Western Europe from the Soviet Union.

34. Dwight D. Eisenhower (1953–1961)

Dwight D. Eisenhower served as the supreme commander of Allied forces in Europe during World War II, overseeing the successful D-Day invasion and the liberation of the continent. As president, Eisenhower oversaw the Korean War. He also led the creation of the modern interstate highway system.

35. John F. Kennedy (1961–1963)

John F. Kennedy, a young and charismatic leader, brought his youthful vigor to the presidency in the early 1960s. In his inaugural address, he famously challenged Americans to "ask not what your country can do for you, but what you can do for your country." He created the Peace Corps and committed the United States to landing astronauts on the Moon by the end of the decade. Tragically, he was assassinated in Dallas, Texas, on November 22, 1963.

36. Lyndon B. Johnson (1963–1969)

Lyndon B. Johnson, a longtime leader in the U.S. Senate and later vice president, ascended to the presidency following the assassination of John F. Kennedy in 1963. Johnson signed a number of landmark laws, including the Civil Rights Act and the Voting Rights Act. He also launched the War on Poverty and significantly increased America's commitment to the Vietnam War.

37. Richard M. Nixon (1969–1974)

Richard M. Nixon, inaugurated in 1969, devoted much of his presidency to winding down the war in Vietnam and renewing U.S. relations with China. Nixon was well respected for his foreign policy knowledge and his ability to deal with the Soviet Union. Despite winning an overwhelming victory in the election of 1972, he was forced to resign from office in 1974 in the wake of the Watergate scandal.

38. Gerald R. Ford (1974–1977)

Gerald Ford became president upon the resignation of Richard Nixon in 1974. His pardon of Nixon was controversial at the time. Ford helped to restore public trust following the Watergate scandal. Nonetheless, he lost his bid for reelection in 1976 to Jimmy Carter.

39. Jimmy Carter (1977–1981)

Jimmy Carter, a peanut farmer, nuclear scientist, and former governor of Georgia defeated incumbent President Gerald Ford in 1976. The Carter administration was challenged with a major energy crisis and economic downturn, as well as a hostage crisis in Iran. Carter lost his own bid for reelection to Ronald Reagan.

40. Ronald Reagan (1981–1989)

Ronald Reagan became president after a successful acting career as well as serving as governor of

California. One of Reagan's most significant goals was to defeat the Soviet Empire. In 1987, he traveled to Berlin, where the Berlin Wall separated communist East Germany from West Germany. Standing at the wall, Reagan famously demanded, "Mr. Gorbachev, tear down this wall!" Two years later, the wall fell—marking the beginning of the end of the Soviet Union.

41. George H. W. Bush (1989–1993)

After serving as Ronald Reagan's vice president, George H. W. Bush was elected the forty-first president of the United States. Bush's presidency was defined by the end of the Cold War and the fall of the Soviet Union, as well as by the First Gulf War, in which the U.S. led a large international coalition to liberate Kuwait.

42. William Jefferson Clinton (1993–2001)

William Jefferson (Bill) Clinton initially sought to make drastic changes to the country's healthcare system. After Republicans won majorities in both chambers of Congress in 1994, Clinton worked with Republicans to pass welfare reform, balance the budget, and cut capital gains taxes. The longest peacetime economic expansion in American history occurred during his presidency. Clinton was the second president to be impeached.

43. George W. Bush (2001–2009)

The presidency of George W. Bush was defined by the terror attacks of September 11, 2001. Following the attacks, Bush led the War on Terror. He was commander in chief through the war in Afghanistan as well as the more controversial war in Iraq. Bush also championed historic income tax cuts, education reforms, and a significant increase in aid to Africa.

44. Barack Obama (2009–2017)

Barack Obama was elected president in 2008, making him the first African American to hold the office. The Affordable Care Act, a healthcare law he advocated, proved to be one of the most controversial issues in recent political history. Obama made expansive use of his authorities as president in many other areas, including immigration, education, and foreign policy.